HEAVYWEIGHT

A BBW & BAD BOY SPORTS ROMANCE

LANA LOVE

LOVE HEART BOOKS

Copyright © 2022 by Lana Love

All rights reserved.

No part of this book may be reproduced in any form or by any electronic or mechanical means, including information storage and retrieval systems, without written permission from the author, except for the use of brief quotations in a book review.

This book is part of the Heartland Heroes series. To read the full series, please visit:

https://www.amazon.com/dp/B0BFRNY6CW

For more Lana Love books, please visit:

https://www.amazon.com/Lana-Love/e/B078KKRB1T/

https://www.loveheartbooks.com

❦ Created with Vellum

CHAPTER 1

BETH

"If I have to tell you one more time, I'm going to break your sorry ass into a million pieces."

"If I want to admire your sister, ain't you or nobody gonna stop me." Dirk looks at my brother, then cuts his eyes to where I'm standing across the boxing gym as if he wants to make sure I'm watching.

He slaps a stupid grin on his face and keeps taunting my brother. Even on a good day, Dirk knows pushing my brother like this is playing with fire. Because the only thing my brother loves more than me is this gym of his—and he would take on an army to save his gym.

My brother lights into Dirk again, and I huff with impatience as he threatens him. I don't know whether to be amused or pissed off that my brother thinks he has a say in who can chase after me and who I can date. It's no mystery that Dirk is a bad boy, but...damn. The man is sexy as sin, and he's been laying on the charm since I've been back. I know all the reasons I shouldn't give him another chance. I also know it's dumb to think his flirting with me means anything. He flirts with all the ring girls who prance around in bikinis, and they fawn all over him. Everyone wants a piece of him.

The man is hotter than a forest fire, but he's also the kind of man you can't hope for a future with. He's all flirting and hot sex, but the minute the R word comes up, he flees before you can blink twice.

"If you think I'm going to let you lead her on a second time, you better consider buying a cemetery plot for yourself."

Dirk broke my heart last year. I came home for summer break and helped Champ balance the books for the gym, and Dirk and I had a hot fling all summer. I foolishly hoped it would develop into something more, that he'd wait for me while I went off for my senior year of college. But when I brought up the subject, he broke up with me instead.

I'd be lying if I said watching my brother threaten him wasn't a little satisfying. Now I'm back and working at the gym, it's weird being around him. I enjoy flirting with him, even if it is a bad idea. I'd never tell Dirk, but I still think about him when I'm in bed. My hand slips under my blankets, and I try to re-create how his fingers made me see stars from coming so hard.

The moment I see my brother's face redden in anger, I know it's time to step in. He's been under strain lately, walking around with a short fuse and dealing with things he won't discuss with me. Plus, there's only so much big brothering I can take before he pisses *me* off.

"Hey, Champ! Back off. Don't you see that I'm right here?"

"Beth..." Champ blinks rapidly as his gaze shifts to me as if he'd forgotten I was here.

"Seriously? What are you going to *try* and warn me about? I know Dirk as well as you do. Better, in fact," I point out.

I'm assaulted by visions of Dirk's arms wrapped around me in bed, making me late for work last summer. I thought it was crazy that Dirk kept coming to my brother's gym after I went back to college because Champ had even more to say about our fling while it was actually happening. I never imagined Dirk would stay around, given how my brother yelled at him.

"Don't you start, too," Champ responds, his muscles relaxing slightly. "I don't want you hurt, little sis, and I remember—" he turns to Dirk with a glower, "how he walked all over you. I'm not going to let him hurt you again. Hell, I should ban him from the gym!"

"Stop being dramatic, Champ. And again," my cheeks burning as my anger flares, "your concern is noted, but it's none of your business. I'm a grown woman, and it's generally accepted that I'm smart. Right?"

"Beth." Champ looks at me, his mouth tightly sealed.

It's not the first time he's been overprotective of me, but I sure wish it would be the last. Anyone else would cower under the weight of my brother's glowering stare, but I roll my eyes, cross my arms over my chest and stare him down.

He hasn't banned Dirk from the gym because Dirk brings in business. Dirk is an up-and-coming heavyweight boxer, and people love to watch him fight. He has that magic combination of natural skill and charisma. If he can get it together and focus, he'll be a boxer who goes down in the history books.

"I can stand here all day like this. You know I'm not lyin'," I snap.

I know I'm young and don't have as much worldly experience, but how am I supposed to learn about myself if someone else is dictating all my choices? I want to live my own life, not what my brother thinks is best for me. If Champ had his way, I'd never have a boyfriend because he doesn't think anyone is good enough for me.

This gets a laugh out of my brother, and just like that, the tension drops from his muscles. He turns and starts to raise his arm, but I reach out and stop him.

"No. My life, my choices. End of discussion."

Champ grunts and stalks off.

"You sure put up a fight for a woman who won't go out with me," Dirk teases, angling his ripped body toward me.

I tremble as his eyes slowly rake over my body, and his eyes linger on my hips – hips he loved to grip those nights we fell into bed. I always showed up at the gym the next day, sleepy and sore but grinning like a fool.

I gasp as the spicy scent of his body reaches me, and I close my eyes and gather up every ounce of my willpower. I remind myself that feeling anything for Dirk is dangerous because he doesn't do relationships. Last summer, a fling was fine for me, but now I want more. I want to meet someone I can settle down with and start a family.

When I open my eyes and see Dirk's hungry green gaze, I want so passionately to say yes. I know he can see my desire, but I also know how fast and hard Champ will beat him into the ground if Dirk breaks my heart. Again.

I turn on my heel, unable to meet his eyes. "I need to get back to work."

~

"Beth," my brother says, the warning evident in his voice.

I've barely been back in the office three minutes, and he comes charging in like I need reprimanding. "Champ, seriously, don't start. I haven't forgotten last summer."

"But—"

"But nothing," I snap, standing to face him and crossing my arms over my chest. "Have you changed your mind about the community fundraiser?"

Champ sighs, and his forehead creases further. He may be a titled boxer, but his old rivalry makes him behave like a stubborn little boy. "You mean with Doyle? Are you out of your mind? I love this town, but it's barely big enough for the two of us. I'll be perfectly content if I never have to see that lousy shithead ever again."

I glance at the old-fashioned hardbound accounting book my brother insists on using. "Things are a little better now Dirk is taking more fights. The finances are still pretty tight."

"I'll figure something out," Champ says, his voice strained.

Thing is, I know he won't. Champ cares about the gym and helping the community. Yet he's as hard-headed as they come, and asking for help has never been his style. He spends more time trying to help people than building his business, and it's like he thinks the universe will magically give him everything he needs. He's had his gym for several years now, but he's run it by the seat of his pants. It might all fall apart if he doesn't make a business plan.

"I don't think you can charge through this like you've done in the past, Champ," I say, softening my voice. "We need to figure out a plan. If not the fundraiser, then…something. You could send Dirk to box, instead. You know he'll sell tickets."

"Hmpf."

"On top of that, it's not going to look good if you're not part of the fundraiser this year. No one in Raytown cares about your beef with Doyle Malone. You need to get past it and do what's right for you and our town."

"Maybe," he grunts and returns to the gym floor. I watch him through the open door, talking to different boxers and offering advice or encouragement. This is his element. As much as he resists starting a family of his own, this gym and all the boxers that come through here? They're his family.

I love my brother. He's gruff and a pain in the ass, but his heart is huge.

Movement catches my eye, and I see Dirk staring right at me. I've been home for a couple of months now, but every time Dirk looks at me, my resolve to keep him at arm's length weakens. Feeling bold, I return his stare, savoring how his full lips curve into a smile as he changes his stance. When he flexes his arm muscles, I bite my lip. My thighs instinctively clench together as familiar, forbidden warmth pools in my core.

Blinking rapidly, I grab the accounts book and focus on the numbers, willing my mind to clear itself of what Dirk's body looks like naked, poised over me in bed, teasing me before making my body vibrate with pleasure.

Why is the man I want most also the one most dangerous to my heart?

CHAPTER 2

DIRK

*L*eaving the ring, I catch Beth from the corner of my eye. She's got a thousand-yard stare going on, which is concerning for someone usually upbeat and cheery.

"Hey, Beth. What's going on? You're a million miles away."

"Oh, Dirk." She looks at me with those blue eyes, and my heart punches against my ribs. "It's... I'll work it out."

"Beth, what's wrong?" The tone of her voice sends a warning.

Getting involved in a woman's life isn't something I do, especially a woman I'm not fucking. But last summer, Beth got under my skin in a way no woman ever has. I still think about her and wrestle with the feelings she stirred up in me. Beth is the closest I've ever gotten to settling down with someone.

Fishing for more information, I ask, "Some guy giving you trouble?" Can't lie. I'd love to beat any man sniffing around her.

"Ah, no," she says, but my question gets a laugh from her. She gives me a long look, and I can see the gears moving in her head. "You want to help?"

"Anything." There isn't a moment's hesitation in my answer. Whatever she needs, I'm there.

"Okay. I need help moving. You might know I'm staying with Champ, but…I need my own space. I found a place, but my car's in the shop. He was supposed to help me, but he says he has some meeting he can't reschedule. He won't tell me what's going on. I want to get it done, and I was set on moving today. You up for it?" The words tumble out of her mouth.

I nod before she even finishes. "Your wish is my command. What time? Back of my truck is empty, so it's ready to go. Do you have much stuff?"

"Not really, no. But Champ is giving me some furniture, so there's that. It's not just boxes."

"Sure," I say, standing a little straighter and flexing my muscles. "Whatever you got, I'm your man."

"Thanks, Dirk. You're a lifesaver."

Seeing the relief on Beth's face makes me happy in a way I can't describe.

"Is this it?" I stack two boxes and head out to my truck, unbelieving that a woman has so little stuff. "I'm not sure why you need help moving."

"You may laugh now," she says, grabbing a lamp and walking with me. "But wait until we get to the basement. There's a big old dresser that needs moving. It's big enough that we might need to wait for Champ to get home."

"I can do it." My voice is gruff at the idea that I can't handle moving a piece of *furniture*. I got this as long as it's not an eight-foot, wood-frame sofa from the 70s. And even if it were, I'd figure out how to get it done. No way in fucking hell do I want to ask for Champ's help, especially in his home. This is his territory. But Beth? I want her to be *my* territory.

"If you say so," she says, shaking her head. "It's okay to ask for help if you need it. I can always get it another day when Champ is here."

"No. I'll make it work. I ain't got all these muscles for nothing."

I push the boxes down the flatbed of my truck, grinning when I hear her muttering, "You sure do have muscles." It gives me hope she'll give me another chance. I've seen her watching me at the gym these last few months. She still feels the chemistry and animal lust we shared last summer. What we shared was hot and fierce, and if I'm honest, she took me by surprise.

When she returned to school, I thought she'd become a memory, and I'd move on to the next string of women. I've never been the committing type. Yet once Beth was gone, I couldn't stop thinking about her, and no matter how many times I tried to look at another woman, no one could live up to Beth. I immediately knew I was a goddamn idiot to have rejected her when she asked for something more. It was then I knew if I had another chance with her, I'd do anything to be with her.

I'm not fucking up this chance.

∼

"Whew!" Beth's cheeks are flushed, and she's panting a little after carrying her bed up the flight of stairs to her apartment.

Grabbing her mattress, I lift and move it easily to the bed, adjusting it until it fits snugly atop the box spring.

"You want to break this thing in?" I sit on the edge of the mattress, smiling at her and patting the space next to me.

When Beth bites her lips, blood roars in my veins, and my cock immediately stiffens. I've been with a lot of women in my time, but not one of them is even half as sexy as Beth when she bites her lip. I want her teeth lightly grazing my skin, then her pink tongue tracing every muscle on my body. The memory of her tongue flicking against my skin makes my heart pound.

"I don't think that's a good idea, Dirk." Beth looks at me, and the battle in her eyes is as plain as day. She hasn't forgotten last summer, either.

We were fucking good together, but then I fucked it up. I liked Beth – a lot – but I flipped when she started talking about the future. An old voice in my head said to pull away because relationships only lead to heartbreak, and I'm not willing to get hurt.

"But it's a fun idea, is it not? Come here."

It feels better than winning a championship belt when she takes my outstretched hand. I pull her toward me, spreading my legs so she can feel how much I still want her.

"My brother will kill both of us if he—"

"Then we don't have to tell him," I whisper in her ear, deeply inhaling her sweet scent.

"But—"

I silence her weak protest with a kiss. At first, she puts her hand on my chest, like she might push me away, but before I can kiss her deeply, she moans and pushes me back on the bed. Her legs find their way over mine, and the touch of her curves is better than I remembered.

She deepens our kiss, and every inch of my body needs her. In a quick move, I wrap my arm around her waist and flip both of us. Her curly brown hair fans out beside her, framing her head and pretty face.

Beth groans and arches her body into mine, running her fingers through my hair and holding my head tightly. One of the sexiest things about Beth was how much she loved fucking and wasn't shy to initiate what she wanted.

My breathing catches when Beth's hands move down my body and fumble at the buttons on my jeans. *Fuck. I've waited a long time for this.*

Her cool hand slides against my skin, her fingertips teasing the base of my hard cock. I push into her hand, but she pulls away, teasing me.

"Oh, is it going to be like that?" I growl, reaching for her hands and pulling them over her head.

I grind my hips against hers, nearly coming hard when she gasps and pushes up against me. Fuck. She's the sexiest woman I've ever even seen. She doesn't hold back.

"Dirk..." Beth's voice is breathless, and her eyes are dilated. Her vulnerability is fucking breathtaking.

"I'm just getting started." I lower my mouth to her perfect pink lips, taking a delicious taste of her mouth. I freeze when a door slams.

"Beth! You here?"

"Let go of me," Beth hisses, fighting under my body in a different way.

I roll off her, standing up quickly to do up my jeans, and watch as Beth quickly checks her clothes and smooths her hair.

"Yeah," she calls out, walking out the bedroom door. Thank fuck this isn't one of those shoebox studio apartments.

"I thought I said I'd help you tomorrow." Champ's voice is impatient, but when isn't it?

"And I said I had a job interview tomorrow."

"I could've helped you on the weekend."

"Champ," Beth says slowly, "I want to live my life on my schedule, not yours. It's fine anyway. Dirk was free and offered to help. We got everything."

"Hey, man." I walk out of her bedroom, bracing myself for whatever fury he's going to unleash on me.

Champ shifts his weight, rocking between his heels and the balls of his feet as if he's preparing to launch himself at me.

I hold up my hands. A fight with Champ would ruin the moment I just shared with Beth, and I don't want to lose that feeling yet. "Don't worry. I'm just on my way out."

"Thanks for your help, Dirk. I owe you one." Beth winks at me.

Suddenly, walking out of her new place is the hardest thing I've ever had to do.

CHAPTER 3

BETH

"You look good today," Champ says as he walks into the office. "What's got you all dressed up? It better not be Dirk. I saw how you two were mooning at each other yesterday."

Champ's voice is laced with exasperation and anger. My cheeks burn with a blush that Champ caught me ogling at Dirk through the office window. Since our kiss when he helped me move, I've wanted him more than I thought it was possible to want someone.

"Seriously, Haywood? Do I have to warn you about meddling in my private life...*again*?" I only use his given name when I'm particularly mad at him, and he knows it. "You need to knock this shit off. I'm a grown woman, and I can make my own decisions, whether they be good or bad. They're mine to make, not yours."

Champ crosses his arms over his chest, shaking his head. "Beth, I care about you. You're my sister. What do you expect me to do?"

"Stop trying to be Dad." My voice softens. Our dad was a roughneck and died in a rig accident when Champ was a teen, and I was in middle school. "Even though I was a kid, he tried to control me like my only value was my virginity and ability to pop out babies."

My brother gives me a long look, and I can see the war in his eyes. Our parents were pretty conservative. I try to be open-minded, and I know Champ tries, too, but when emotions flare, we go back to our parents and how we were as children.

"Beth," Champ says, taking a deep breath, "you know I love you. But come on. Dirk? He doesn't deserve a woman like you. All he's good with is boxing. I don't think he knows how to treat a woman," he coughs and lowers his voice, "outside the bedroom."

"Whatever," I say, knowing I sound bratty. "And I'm dressed up because I have a job interview this afternoon. I told you about this."

"I didn't think you were serious."

"I am. Now get out of here so I can finish up before I head out."

Champ grumbles but leaves and closes the door to the office behind him.

As I watch him, I think about what he said. In truth, I can't disagree with my brother. I'm not sure Dirk would know love if it bit him in the ass. But. There was...*something* in the air when Dirk helped me move, and we fell onto my bed. Again. I know what pure lust feels like, and that isn't what I feel with Dirk. Yes, plenty of lust in the air, but there...there was more. Through all his swagger, there were hints of something deep and tender. That's not how a guy is when all he wants is to get laid. I'm familiar with men who look at me and my heavy curves and decide I'd be up for a good time and nothing else.

Dirk looks at me with lust, but sometimes it seems like something more. Like he's all lathered up because of *me*, not because I'm a woman who happens to be in the room with him.

I know we have lust when we're together. But could we have more?

"Hey, Champ!" I call out to my brother, who's standing in the ring with Caleb. He's giving him advice on shifting the weight on his feet and timing his punches with his body movements.

"What's up, Beth? I thought you were heading out." Champ grabs a bottle of water and downs it. His eyes flicker for a moment as they land on Opal, but then the wall comes down, and he turns to me.

"I am, in a few minutes. This is Opal. I'm not sure if you've met before. In any case, she's here on behalf of the fire department. They've got another—"

"You can tell that son of a bitch to—"

"Champ," I say, my voice a warning. "You know you need to do this. What does it say about helping the community if you won't do the charity fight?"

"More than I already am?" My brother puts on an air of arrogance, but he knows what I'm talking about. He's too freaking proud to do a charity fight because he claims Doyle cheated in their last fight, which Champ lost.

"Champ, please."

"No. And that's final." Champ doesn't wait for a response before turning and stalking away.

"Sorry about that." I shrug. "But that's about what I expected his response would be. I've been trying to talk to him about it, but," I gesture toward Champ's retreating back, "you can see how well that goes."

"Do you think you can convince your brother?" Opal gives me a hopeful look.

"I…" I glance out to the ring, where Champ is coaching Caleb. "I'd like to think I could convince him to say yes, but he's…hardheaded."

"Oh, yeah. My brother will be disappointed, but you're right about Dirk. Is your brother that stuck in the past?" Opal asks in surprise.

I laugh. "Girl, you don't even want to know. He can hold a grudge like nobody's business. You think *I'm* stubborn? You saw him just now. He's just like our father. We grew up in a family where it was weak to back down. I've learned better, but Champ doesn't like change and doesn't compromise easily."

"My brother is going to have a field day, you know," Opal says, laughing and shaking her head. "He still crows to anyone who'll listen about when he beat your brother. If Champ won't fight, Doyle will go around saying Champ is too scared to fight him, that he's lost his fire."

I take a deep breath as I listen to Opal. She's not wrong. As I make a mental note to talk to Champ and see if I can change his mind, I notice how Opal looks at my brother with longing.

"You're not wrong, Opal. I can try and talk to him again later, but I can't make any promises. However, I do have a suggestion. How about we put Dirk in the fight? I've already suggested it to Champ. You know Dirk will draw a crowd for sure."

"I know Antonia and Colleen were hoping for your brother, but I'll float the idea."

"Cool. I know it's not the same, but it'd still be a good fight. I reach out and hold her arm when she takes a step forward. "I have an entirely different question. I see how you look at my brother."

"What?" Opal flusters and glances away from Champ, but her eyes keep returning to him. "It's…"

I laugh as she tries to cover up her emotions, and then I put my arm through hers. "If you're interested, you should ask him out."

"What?" A look of alarm passes over my friend's face. "I could never do that! He's never looked twice at me. I don't even know why he would."

"Girl, don't sell yourself short. You're a total babe."

"But…he hates my twin brother. I'm also half his age."

"He's not that old." I laugh. "But you're right about your brother. I'm not sure he realizes you're his twin. I wouldn't mention that right away."

LANA LOVE

Opal's gaze flicks over my shoulder, and she grins. "That man is looking at you like you're a snack."

"What?" I follow Opal's gaze, and my mouth falls open.

There, in the doorway to the gym, is Dirk. He's wearing pressed jeans and a tight black t-shirt that strains against his muscles. I think he even got a haircut because his normally unruly hair is slicked back.

"You got a thing going on?" Opal lightly bumps her shoulder into mine.

I can help but smile. Dirk didn't make this much effort during our fling when I was home from college last summer. We weren't fucking all the time, but we knew I was only around for the summer. It was a different vibe, when I thought it was just a summer fling.

"I... Maybe. We had a thing last summer, and he's asked me out again."

"Girl, he looks serious. Wait," Opal pauses, turning her attention to me. "This is the guy from last summer. *That* guy?"

"Yeah."

"Oh, wow. He cleans up real nice. Do you think you have a future?"

"I'm not sure. Probably not. But he's hard to say no to." I look over at Dirk, who hasn't taken his eyes off me since I saw him. Champ's warning echoes in my mind, but the thumping of my heart and the look in Dirk's eyes answer the question. "Anyway, I should get going. I have a job interview over at the bank."

Opal smiles. "Good luck."

CHAPTER 4

DIRK

"Look." Champ waits for one of the guys to unlace our gloves and take them off. "I'm not going to lie. You're good. You're really good."

Praise from Champ is rare. I smile and stand straighter, letting it all go to my head. "Of course I'm good—"

"And all you'll ever be is *good* unless you get your shit together." Champ's voice is harsh.

Deep down, he's only saying what I don't like to admit. I have natural talent, but I know I'm only kidding myself by thinking I don't need to train as hard as the other guys.

"You need to buckle down and do the work. It's obvious you're not training as hard as you need to. If you don't train, you'll lose."

The happiness from his praise fizzles to mush. I know I haven't been training as much as Champ has instructed. It's hard work, and I can't get past the desire to be good at something without much effort. Boxing has always been fun, and it turned out I was good at it. But I have to start training if I want to get to the next level and stay there.

"Dirk. Pay attention to me." Champ's voice is stern, and it immediately snaps my attention back to him.

"Sorry, Champ."

"Don't be sorry. Focus. Focus on training. Focus on each fight. If you want to move on and build a career, you have to win this."

"You want me to represent the gym?" This is big. Fighting Doyle is a big deal. He and Champ have history, and it's not the friendly kind.

The gravity of Champ's words cut through everything and sink deep. I love boxing. It's what I want to do for as long as I can. But he's right – I'm not going anywhere unless I stop fucking around and put in the work. Champ is the best coach in the Heartland region, and if I screw up here, I'll never make it big.

"I'll do better. I swear."

"Yeah, you will. And one more thing." Champ takes a step closer and the tension rolling off his body is impossible to miss.

"Yeah?" I lift my chin. I know what's coming.

"Stay the fuck away from my sister." His voice is a menacing growl.

I stop smirking when I see his jaw tighten and twitch with poorly disguised anger. While I can appreciate him being protective of Beth, doesn't he realize the more he tells me to stay away, the more I won't? "The choice is Beth's, not yours. If she—"

"Don't give me any of that!" Champ explodes in anger, his hands balling into fists. "I know Beth. She deserves more than a fighter who can't even commit to the fight. If you can't do that, why would you commit to her? If you don't stay away from Beth, I'll kick you out of the gym."

My frustration with Champ fuels my fists as I pound the punching bag.

I get that he doesn't want me chasing Beth because she's his little sister. I'd be protective of her, too. But how am I supposed to stay away from her? Last summer, I knew there was something special about her, but she was only home for a few months, and I wasn't sure I'd ever see her again. It was hard to say goodbye to her, but I couldn't give her what she wanted.

Truth is, Champ and I have always butted heads. Yet he's the best boxing coach, and I need him.

"Yo, Dirk!" Caleb yells, stepping away from the bag.

"What?" My voice is a sharp bark as I shake my arms out and work to catch my breath. I have the distinct impression he's been talking to me, but I haven't heard a word he's said.

"I said, do you want to come out with the guys and me tonight? There's a band playing down at the Roadhouse. Gonna be a lot of chicks there."

I start to nod, but then I realize I don't want to go. I don't want to chase girls with Caleb and the guys. I'm tired of that. Beth being back has me thinking about what it'd be like to settle down with a woman – with her. It's not something I've ever done, and the idea scares the ever-loving shit out of me, but I don't even want to *look* at another woman.

"Nah, man. I'm gonna pass on this one."

"What?" Caleb laughs, reaching out to touch my forehead. "You got a fever? I bet we could find one of the nurses there. Take your temperature and see what's wrong. Maybe play a little doctor and nurse."

"Nah," I say, stalling. I know better than to talk about Beth with another one of the boxers. I still have to get a handle on my emotions. "Just need a night off."

"You still chasing after Beth? I heard Champ lit into you last week." Caleb glances toward the gym office, but the door is closed.

"I like her," I finally admit, "but I don't know if anything will come of it. She's special, though. She's fucking amazing."

Caleb looks at me, a more thoughtful look in his eyes. "Then you better man up and figure it out. Girl like that ain't gonna be single for long around here."

I nod at Caleb because I know he's right.

I've seen a few of my buddies get married in the last year. They all swore they would never willingly tie themselves to one woman, but then that special woman came along, and everything changed. They couldn't get enough of her, and then they were proposing and walking down the aisle, giving themselves to the woman forever. The rest of us gave them shit, but the truth is, they're all happier than I've ever seen them.

I want that happiness in my life. And I want it with Beth.

CHAPTER 5

BETH

"Beth Hopkins! As I live and breathe!"

My hand freezes in midair while I'm reaching for another case of bottled water for the gym. I spin, and I can't help but scream in happiness. "Oh, my God! Luann! I thought you left town!"

Other shoppers in Heartland Food Mart turn and stare at us, but I don't care. Luann was one of my closest friends before we left for college, and I haven't seen her in ages. She's barely on social media, and I thought she was gone when I came back.

"I will be soon. I got the traveling nurse job. I need to get out and see the world a little." She's still smiling when she says this, but some of the brightness in her eyes dims. I know there's a story, but it's not one to ask about in a crowded grocery store.

"I know this is last-minute, but what are your plans right now? Do you want to grab a bite at The Busy Bee?"

She smiles, and her eyes light up again. "That would be nice."

"Cool. I need to drop this water off at the gym. Do you mind tagging along?" I hoist two more cases of bottled water into my cart.

"Not at all. How's your brother doing?"

"Same as ever." I sigh. "Still acting like my dad. Still trying to take care of everyone but himself."

"Uh, oh." Luann laughs and rolls her eyes. "You dating someone new?"

"Maybe?"

It takes until we get to the gym for me to finish filling Luann in on everything going on with Dirk.

"Girl, you got it bad."

"What? No!" I blush and look away, but a voice deep inside me says that maybe Luann is right.

"I remember the way you two were last summer. And Beth, the way you're talking about him now? No matter how much you want to try and convince yourself otherwise, what you had was more than a fling."

"Then how come he disappeared when I suggested maybe we could have something more?"

"Because he's an idiot? Most men are."

The sounds and scent of sweaty men greet us as Luann and I carry the flats of bottled water into the gym.

"Beth! Let me give you a hand."

Dirk is next to me before I realize it, lifting the flats of water from Luann and my arms. He winks at me as he takes them toward the storage closet.

"Girl, I want someone who looks at me the way he looks at you. He lit up when he saw you."

"Luann!" My voice is a hiss. Last thing I need is for the other boxers to hear that I'm talking about Dirk to my friends. That is a level of teasing I do not need in my life.

"I'm serious. He was obviously showing off for you."

"Maybe," I say, though I know she's right. Every time I enter the gym, he does something to catch my eye or makes an excuse to come and talk to me. I'm not used to men showing off for me like this.

"Oh! Champ!" Luann calls out to my brother and waves him over.

"Hey, Luann. How are you?" Champ nods at her, touching her shoulder lightly in greeting.

"Champ, it's good to see you. Can we, uh, can we talk somewhere private?"

Champ raises an eyebrow, and I shrug when he looks at me. I have no idea what business she might have with him.

Once we're in the office with the door closed, Luann sighs.

"I'll get to the point. My sister, Shelley, she's…she's having problems with her boyfriend. She throws him out, then he comes round with flowers and fake promises, and she takes him back."

"Go on," Champ prompts Luann when she falls silent. His fingers flex. I think we both know where this is going.

"This guy... He hits her sometimes."

"Motherfucker!" Champ's outrage is instant. He may be old-fashioned, but he has a zero-tolerance policy for violence against women. "We can take care of that for you," he adds, his tone dark.

"No, no. That's not what I meant," Luann says quickly. "She wants to leave him for good, but she gets scared. I wanted to ask if you could give her some self-defense lessons, so she can stand up to him and protect herself. She's strong in so many ways, but not when it comes to this asshole. Pardon my language."

Champ shakes his head. "No apology needed. We don't have a class like that, but we will. It won't take much to set that up. I'll have one of the guys lead it. No charge. Beth and I will work out the details, and she'll let you know."

Luann audibly exhales, and she half-smiles at Champ. "Thanks so much. It might take her a while to come in, but I'll make sure she does. It's...she has a hard time with men. She's too trusting."

Champ's head jerks at the sound of two boxers yelling at each other, and he moves toward the office door. "I gotta run. But don't worry. Whatever you need, you got. And I'm serious if you need help dealing with this asshole. Real men don't hit women."

"I don't mean to be a broken record," Luann says, motioning to the waitress for our check, "but you need to re-think how you feel about Dirk."

"Luann, I don't know—"

"No, Beth, hear me out. You've just told me about how hot and heavy you were two last summer. Seeing the two of you together, today? It was like looking at raw lightning."

I laugh. "That, my dear friend, was lust. Pure, unbridled lust."

"Beth, no." Luann shakes her head. "If that's what you think, you don't see what I see. Even today, when we went into the gym, he was watching you something fierce. And no," she holds up her hand to stop me from talking, "it wasn't just lust. There was a fierce tenderness in his eyes like he was looking at someone precious to him that he's scared of losing."

I stare at Luann, unsure of what to think. The thought sends shivers across my skin. I'd give him a chance if I thought Dirk was ready to settle down. He's strong, talented, and sexy as sin, and he makes me feel desirable, despite my weight. He could have any woman he wants, especially the slim ring girls in their shiny bikinis, but Luann is right – he's chasing after me.

Could Luann be right? Could something serious develop with Dirk?

CHAPTER 6

DIRK

Once again, Floyd nearly knocks me flat on my ass.

"Man, what's wrong with you? I don't mind whooping your ass, but I want it to be a fair win. I thought you were some hotshot boxer. What's wrong with you?"

"I'm distracted. That's all," I say, ignoring what might be an insult.

Floyd and I leave the ring and walk over and grab some bottled water. I take a long drink and shake out my limbs, but I can't loosen the tension building inside me. It's not the same tension as before a fight, but a deeper tension wrapped around my soul.

"Dirk, my man!" Caleb calls, grinning as he comes out of the locker room. "You and Floyd want to join me for some brews tonight?"

Floyd nods. "Yeah, I'm in for that. Not much boxing going on here."

There's a challenge in Floyd's voice, but I ignore it. I don't know Floyd well yet but dealing with him is not my priority. "Nah, count me out. I got some stuff to take care of."

"Your loss, man." Caleb grins. "I need to get my dick wet tonight. You good to be my wingman, Floyd? You're not going to be a bastard and cockblock me, are you?"

Floyd laughs. Maybe he's a decent guy, after all. We don't need anyone here with a stick up their ass. I was starting to wonder about Floyd.

"Yeah, I got you. I'm not the dating type."

Caleb raises an eyebrow at Floyd. "Get your ass cleaned up, then."

I pace around the gym, thankful it's quiet now. All the other boxers are gone, though Champ has been on the phone in the office for what seems like half the day. Beth said he was up to something, and she's right. Champ is a man who hates talking on the phone, so whatever has him locked in his office must be important.

After I see Caleb and Floyd leave, I make my way over to the battered speed bag. Dancing around on my feet, I warm my muscles up again. I start a slow rhythm of hits, then pick up the pace until the bag moves at a fast, steady rhythm and my muscles are pumping.

"You're looking good there."

I jump at the sound of Champ's voice. He's standing there with his arms crossed over his chest as he observes me.

"You shittin' me?" I grab a towel and wipe the sweat from my face and neck.

"I'm not. What are you doing here anyway? Shouldn't you be out with Caleb?"

"I decided to stay and practice some more." Don't know why, but I suddenly feel like I've been called in front of the school principal. I know it's not like me to stay late like this, but between my friends getting married and Beth coming back, I realize I need to get my shit together and make something more of my life.

"Good. If you want to do the fundraiser fight, it's yours." Champ's voice is gruff, but he smiles at me.

"You serious?" You want me to represent the gym?" This is big. Fighting Doyle is a big deal. He and Champ have history, and it's not the friendly kind.

The gravity of Champ's words cut through everything and sink deep. I love boxing. It's what I want to do for as long as I can. But he's right – I'm not going anywhere unless I stop fucking around and put in the work. Champ is the best coach in the Heartland region, and if I screw up here, I'll never make it big.

"Very. Just keep training and ask for help if you need it. I'm glad you're working harder. It's how you're going to keep winning. I don't want losers in my gym. You got potential, but you gotta put in the work. Understand?"

"Yes, sir." Praise from Champ doesn't come easy, and it makes me double down on my belief that this is the right thing to do. If I'm going to succeed in the ring and with Beth, I need to do the work to make those things a reality.

With sweat dripping off me and sore muscles, I go into the locker room to change. As I pack my gear, I realize I have to follow my heart, no matter how scary it seems. There are so many reasons to stay away from Beth, not least because Champ will pound me to a pulp and ban me if I hurt her again. Yet the more I see her, the more I know that walking away isn't a fucking option.

Beth came in late today, and she avoided me. Every time I try to get close to her, she got skittish and disappeared. Yet every time I look at her, there's something in her eyes and it looks like what I feel in my heart. It's like we're in the ring, dancing around each other, waiting for the other person to make the first move.

Beth isn't just another girl. Sure, she's sexy as fuck because how could any man not find her thick body seductive? I dream about her thick thighs locked around my head as I eat her sweet pussy.

But she's more than that. She's a hell of a lot sexier than the ring girls. She's smart and thinks for herself, and I respect that. She understands boxing, and I don't have to explain what fighting means to me.

I've spent a long time chasing around for good fucks and a good time. But now? I've watched my buddies getting married, and I see there's more to life. I want love in my life. It's not something I ever expected or thought I'd find, but I can't turn away from it.

The only things important in my life are boxing and Beth. I'm going to fight to make her mine.

CHAPTER 7

BETH

"I'm calling for Beth Hopkins."

"This is Beth."

I recognized the number the second it appeared on my phone screen. My heart pounds like a drum in my chest. *Please let them offer me the job!*

"Hi, Beth. I thought that was you. This is Lois Barton from Heartland Bank and Savings. Do you have a moment?"

"Absolutely. It was great to meet you last week. Did you have more questions for me?"

Lois chuckles. "Beth, the only question we have is when can you start? We were all extremely impressed with your interview. You don't have a lot of experience, but you have enthusiasm, and your degree swayed us. Would you like to come work with us at Heartland Bank and Savings?"

"Yes! Thank you so much!" I pace around my new apartment, pumping my arm in the air.

The bank was my first choice for a job, and this offer is a dream come true. I'll start as a Customer Account Specialist, which is a fancy way of saying I'll help people open accounts and prepare cashier's checks. Lois said in my interview that they like to develop long-term relationships with their employees, which means they do a lot of training to promote good employees to higher jobs.

"That's wonderful, Beth. We're looking forward to having you come on board. HR will send you some paperwork to fill out, and they'll coordinate with you for a start date. Now, you said you were working at Champ's Gym currently. How much notice do you need to give?"

I take a deep breath to try and calm down a little. "Champ is my brother, so there is some flexibility."

"That's good to hear. Everyone is eager to get you started right away, but we understand you need to give notice and not leave your brother in the lurch. Again, welcome aboard! We're looking forward to you joining our team. I hope we have a long relationship together."

"Me, too, Lois. I'll keep an eye out for the paperwork and return it to you ASAP. Thanks again!"

After our call, I scream a little and dance around my apartment. Everything is falling into place with my life. Finished college. Moved into my own apartment. Landed my dream job.

I just wish I could trust my feelings for Dirk. There's no doubting the magnetism between us, but I want more than hot lust. I need a man I can trust with my heart.

LANA LOVE

"Champ, hey." I walk into the gym office. I can't help but chuckle when I see Champ bent over the laptop, pecking at the keys with a single finger.

"What's up, sis?"

"I need to talk to you." I close the office door and stand up straighter. It's a given that Champ isn't going to like me leaving, but he needs to understand how much this means to me.

"Well..." My resolve wavers. I was so confident and sure of myself, but now, I'm reverting to Champ's Little Sister and not Beth the Grown Woman.

"Spit it out. I gotta session with that new guy, Floyd." Irritation flashes across his eyes.

"Hey, you okay?"

Champ grunts and pushes the laptop closed. "It's this fundraiser."

"You changed your mind about boxing?"

"And go up against that cheater, Doyle?" Champ's laugh is a sharp bark, and he rubs his hand over his face. "No, I haven't changed my mind. Dirk can fight him or whoever he sends in his place. Not my problem."

I look at Champ and nod, sensing how upset he is. He's never told me the full story, but I know he and Doyle both served in the Army together. They competed in a boxing match, and unexpectedly, Doyle won. Champ had been undefeated until then, and his pride has never recovered. If there was a competition for holding a grudge, Champ would win hands down.

"But enough of that. What did you want to talk about?"

"I got the job."

"What job? You're working here."

"Champ. You knew me being here was temporary. I love you, but I need to stand on my own two feet."

"What's the job?" Champ sighs and crosses his arms over his chest.

"It's at the bank. I told you it was the job I wanted. I'll start as a Customer Account Specialist, but they'll train me to be a loan officer. They were my first choice." It's impossible for me to hide my excitement.

Champ scowls at me. "Loans? You'll be a part of the financial machine that strangles people?"

I sigh impatiently. "They're not loan sharks. I'm eventually going to be a loan *officer* in the mortgage division. Helping people buy a home is what I want to do."

Champ stares at me, and I can see everything starting to sink in for him. He slumps almost imperceptibly and nods. "So you're leaving me high and dry?" There's a sharp frustration in his voice.

"I can help you out on the weekends, but I can't do your books for you like I have been. You'll either need to do it yourself or hire someone to help you."

"I don't want a stranger in here." Champ crosses his arms over his chest and stands up to his full height.

"This is non-negotiable," I say, standing straighter and looking Champ in the eyes. "I can help you find someone, but I'm not going to work here forever."

When Champ growls my name, I lose my patience.

"Champ, I love you, but you need to treat me like an adult. You don't get to dictate my love life or my job. I need you to respect my choices. Do you get it?"

Champ shifts his weight as he stares me down, but eventually he nods. "I don't have to tell you I don't like it, but I'll respect your decision to work at the bank. You have my permission."

"Your *permission*? Are you freaking kidding me? I'm not asking for your permission, Haywood Hopkins." Fury leaks out of my voice as I glare at my brother. "You do not control my life," I say slowly, enunciating each word.

"Beth, I'm trying to look out for you."

Frustrated anger boils up in me. "How? By dictating my life? You don't seem to understand the difference between controlling and supportive. You don't get to make all my decisions, even if you think you're saving me from making a mistake. Can't you let me make my own choices – good or bad – and support me? I need you to let me live my life. Can you do that?"

My voice is shrill, which annoys me, but I can't help it. There's too much going on, and the thought that my brother won't be there to support me when I'm doing well or something goes wrong slices so deeply into my heart that my emotions are a mess.

Champ stares at me for a long time, and I'm scared he won't compromise. What would I do without my brother?

"I'm sorry, Beth," he says, eventually. "Is it wrong that I like having you here or that I want this to be a family business?"

I can't help but laugh. "This place is *Champ's* Gym, not the Hopkins' Family Gym. Do you have plans to change the name?"

"Oh, hell…" Champ tries to hide a smile. "Okay. I get your point. But you have to understand that I want what's best for you."

"And what's best for *you*," I tease. "You can't keep an eye on me twenty-four-seven. I'll still be around to help out…*a little*, but you need to hire someone."

"I'll consider it." Champ's voice is gruff, but there's a reluctant acceptance in his eyes.

"I'm glad to hear that. Are we good?" I'm pretty sure we are, but I need to hear him say it.

"Of course, we are, Beth. We're family." Champ looks at me like he's surprised I'm asking. Times like this, I can't tell if I'm blowing things out of proportion or not. "I'll always be here for you, even if it's to point out how you're making a decision that goes against common sense." He laughs.

"That sounds about right," I say, rolling my eyes.

I walk over to him and stand on my toes to give him a bear hug. He grumbles when I wrap my arms around him tightly, but he can't hide his sigh and hugs me back. We may spar and fight, like the guys in the gym, but Champ is family. To make my way in the world, I have to move past that safety and make my own decisions.

"Thanks, Champ. Love you." I squeeze him again, grateful that he came around. "I'm going to go get some lunch, but I'll come back and finish up the accounts payable."

Champ nods, and I can see he really is okay with accepting my choices. "Love you, too, little sis." We step apart and smile at each other, and I feel the love between us strengthen and expand. "Now get out of here before I change my mind."

I huff and turn to leave, but I'm laughing as I do. "Whatever."

CHAPTER 8

DIRK

"Yo, Dirk," Caleb says. I turn back to him and see him dropping his arms.

"What? Sorry, man." It seems like every time Beth talks to her brother, they're arguing. I want to go to her and stand up to Champ when I see it happen. He can be a scary motherfucker, and even though Beth stands up to him, I still want to stand between them.

"Champ is going to yell at you if he sees you're watching his sister again instead of training," Caleb points out. "Your fight isn't some shoo-in, you know. Doyle doesn't box much these days, but he's as good as Champ, and he'll knock you on your ass if you're not in top form and paying fucking attention."

"Yeah, sorry, Caleb. You're right." Frustration hits me like a sucker punch. Champ has told me if I don't buckle down, I won't make it further than I already have, but it's only now starting to sink in.

"Dude, you have to decide what's more important – chasing Champ's sister or training for your fight. What's it going to be?"

Caleb is exasperated, and I don't blame him. Everyone at Champ's Gym is committed to boxing, but I've only been skating by with the bare minimum.

Looking back toward the office, the sight of Beth and Champ hugging is odd but reassuring. They've worked out their differences.

"It's going to be both," I say, bouncing on the balls of my feet and lifting my gloves. "So let's get back to it. I won't be distracted again."

∼

"Hey, Champ. Beth around?" As soon as I finished sparring with Caleb, I went to the locker room for a quick shower and got dressed. I'm not in fancy duds, but they'll have to do.

Champ narrows his eyes as he looks at me. "She's probably still at the diner, getting lunch. Something I can help you with?"

The challenge in Champ's voice is unmistakable. Truth is, I'd take anything he threw at me. I'd rather not get beaten to a pulp by the brother of the woman I love, but if that's the price I have to pay, no question I'd pay up. She's worth anything Champ wants to dish out to me.

"Nah, I'll catch up with her. Thanks, man."

I turn and leave, hoisting my bag over my shoulder as I walk down the sunny street toward the diner. All the words I want to say to Beth jumble in my mind. Do I just tell her I love her? Do I ask her to go steady? I have no fucking idea what I'm doing because I've never had this talk with a woman. It's always been "thanks, I'll call you," with me rarely calling a woman. Beth is the only woman I've ever wanted to invest real time and effort in.

No, that's not right. I already know I want more than going steady. I want her forever, but I don't know how to say it without sounding like a fool. I want to break down the wall between us and build something greater with her.

Before I know it, I'm standing in front of The Busy Bee diner. I look in the large window, smiling as I see Beth laughing with the waitress, Janice. Her amusement at whatever Janice is saying is pure and unfiltered, her face open. That. That is the face I want to see every day for the rest of my life. I want to make her smile like that, to laugh with pure delight.

"What are you doing here?" The light in Beth's eyes changes, and even though she's wary, she can't hide the longing in them. "Did Champ send you to find me?"

"No," I say, taking a seat across from her. I place my hands flat on the table to steady them because, for once in my life, I'm nervous. Going into a fight is easier than sitting across from the woman I love and gambling on whether she'll agree to be my girl.

"Then what's up? If you're going to try and ask me out again..." Her voice trails off and she looks down. Her face is resolute yet sad when she looks back at me. "It's just... We're not meant to be."

I hold up my hand to stop her from saying more. I'm not surprised she's thought about this. Since she's been back, she's been all I can think about. "I know you said no, but I can't accept that. I want you in my life, Beth. There's no doubt in my mind you're the woman for me. I know I have a bad reputation, but I've never found a woman like you. You make me realize that a life together is better than a life alone. I don't want a mundane life. I want to be with you. I'll take whatever your brother throws at me. You're worth it. I promise I won't hurt you. It would kill me to hurt you. I…I love you."

The words leave my mouth in a nervous rush like a fucking teenager, like if I don't say them all at once, I won't be able to. For the first time in a long time, I'm uncertain about something I need – and I need Beth.

"Dirk…I…" She pauses and shakes her head.

I wait with a patience that's unnatural to me. I'm dying to know what she'll say.

It takes her a minute before she speaks again. "I like you, Dirk, I do," she says, but there's a sad sigh in her voice.

"Then what's the problem? You don't sound excited." My heart thumps in my chest. Is this what the beginning of heartbreak looks like?

"Dirk, I know you." Beth spins her water glass in a circle on the table and leans against the booth. "You want me because I'm not falling over myself trying to seduce you."

"Beth, it's more than that. You're not just a conquest."

"Why should I think you've changed? I've seen you staring at the ring girls." Beth's eyes cut away, and her voice catches. "That's not the kind of woman I am, and I never will be."

"Beth Hopkins, look at me." I pause, waiting for her to lift her head and meet my eyes. When she does, the expression on her face is wary. "I don't want a ring girl. I want you. They're not sexy like you."

She laughs, but I hold up my hand so I can continue speaking.

"They're not smart like you. Believe me, Beth, I've met a lot of women in my life, but no one has me wanting more like you do. I want to build something lasting with you. Fuck." Despite my tense muscles, I slouch in the booth and run my hand over my face. "Beth, I'll be honest with you. I don't know how to do this relationship thing. But I want to – with *you*. Only with you. Forever with you."

Something softens in Beth's eyes, and adrenaline vibrates through my body. She relaxes a little and leans toward me, her eyes intent upon mine. "Are you serious, Dirk Walden?"

"Serious as a fucking heart attack."

"What about my brother?" A grin pulls at Beth's mouth.

I feel like I'm at the end of a match. On the verge of winning. Victory pumping through my veins with the knowledge that nothing can stop me from getting what I want. "Beth, I'm going to stand my ground and take whatever he dishes out. I know he's your brother but being with me is your choice. You get to choose what and who you want in your life."

Beth breaks into a big smile and reaches across the table for my hand, pulling me close. "Kiss me."

CHAPTER 9

BETH

"Whatcha thinking about, babe?" Dirk tightens his arm around my shoulders as we walk down the street.

I couldn't be happier. He may think I don't notice, but I know he's pushing out his chest and strutting as we make our way back to my apartment. Watching Dirk show off fills my heart with happiness and takes my breath away.

This is real. It's really happening.

When Dirk tracked me down at the diner and professed his love for me, I kept pinching myself to see if it was real. Everything I've wanted since last year is coming true.

"You," I say simply and smile.

Dirk arches his eyebrow, and the wicked smile on his lips fuels the fire that's been burning inside me since our kiss at the diner.

"Good thoughts, I hope?" he asks with a hint of vulnerability.

I remember what he said about never having a real relationship before. I don't have much experience, but I know how scary it is to open up to someone you care about. It's scary for me, too.

"Very good thoughts." I reach up and run my hand across my chest.

Mine. He's mine.

I look at Dirk, grinning like an idiot, and I don't care. I've had girlfriends who told me stories about withholding affection or never revealing how much they like someone, but I'm not like that. I can't hide how happy Dirk makes me.

"Do some of those thoughts involve us spending some time in your new bed?" Dirk's eyes drop to my lips.

I instinctively raise my face to him, hungry for his kiss. "They sure do," I breathe, gasping as his lips graze mine.

By the time we make it to my place and we're standing in my bedroom, the air between us is electric. Every glance, every touch sends currents of pleasure straight to my core.

"This is your last chance to back out," I tease, though I already know he won't.

"The fuck I will." Dirk's voice is gruff as he pulls me against his muscular body. "I may not have experience with relationships, but I'm gonna learn. You make me want things I never knew I wanted, Beth."

Dirk's voice wavers, and my heart trembles at his emotion. He has such a tough persona because showing vulnerability means your opponent has an advantage. I understand what it means that he's doing this – he's showing me he trusts me and is committed to me, to us.

"Good. Because I'm not letting you go, either."

Our lips meet in a frantic, hot kiss. Dirk's teeth nip at my lips and graze my skin, making me shiver with need. Even though we know each other's bodies and how to bring each other pleasure, everything feels new. I let myself experience a new set of emotions – this isn't a summer fling filled with fun and fucking. This is more. This is opening our lives up to each other and forging ahead together.

I push Dirk onto the bed and frantically tug at his jeans, but he lifts his hips and pushes them down himself. And then he's naked on my bed, his thick cock already standing at attention. My mouth waters as he flexes his muscles. As I start to undress, he stands and puts his hands over mine.

"Allow me." Dirk's voice is a husky whisper against my neck as his hands roam over my body, and he presses himself against me from behind.

"Dirk," I moan. "I need you."

"Beth, babe. I'm not going to rush this." He slips my shirt over my head and places his fingers under my bra strap. My body squirms against his, urgent need blinding me. "We know we're good in bed. I'm gonna make love to you."

Love fills my heart, and I don't know if I can hold all this emotion inside me. All at once, I know this is going to last. We're not going to be future exes. This, right here, right now, is sealing our future.

Dirk trails kisses over my skin as he carefully and slowly undresses me. My body shakes with unmet need as his fingertips and lips roam over my body.

Dirk guides me back to bed, holding his strong body over mine. He wiggles his hips so his cock is deliciously close to my core.

"You're teasing me." My voice is a whine. I press my body against his, but he raises out of reach.

"I could get used to seeing you like this. Do you realize how fucking sexy you are, squirming below me, aching for my cock?"

"You said you were going to make love to me." My breath is a hot whisper as he lowers his mouth to mine and his tongue forcefully invades my mouth. My tongue massages his, and pleasure ripples through me when he shudders and moans into my mouth.

"What do you want, Beth?" Dirk's green eyes glisten, his mouth parted with desire.

"I need you to make love to me."

"Beth…" Dirk's voice is a thick groan as he thrusts deep inside me, filling me in the way only he can. There is nothing so perfect as how our bodies fit together. "Fuck, you are so goddamn beautiful."

Dirk's eyes search mine, and my heart aches at the raw need and desire in them. I wrap my arms around him, licking and sucking at his neck as he makes love to me so passionately that I can already feel the rawness forming. I arch my back and bear down on this cock, my body and soul yearning for our pleasure.

Dirk wraps one arm around my back and I giggle with surprise as he rolls us over so I'm on top. I sit up and lace my fingers through his, and he steels his arms as my support as my body takes over. I grind over him, his cock fully buried inside me, stroking my g-spot so perfectly that my explosion is seconds away.

"I can't wait…" My hips move faster and faster, unable to slow down. My core is on fire as we rock together, so loud my new bed scrapes harshly again the hardwood floor.

"Don't wait, babe. Come with me." Dirk's eyes are wild as he looks up at me, thrusting fast and deep.

He lifts his head and takes one of my straining nipples in his mouth, his tongue sucking and flicking it. I close my eyes and see fireworks exploding as a hot, hard rush of pleasure breaks through my body. I scream his name, my hips bouncing on him as my orgasm shatters and I come hard.

Dirk's body bucks and shakes under mine. "Beth!" he yells, holding me so tight that it feels like we're one person.

We collapse, panting, our hands never leaving each other. Dirk doesn't let go of me as we lay in bed, grinning like idiots as we stare into each other's eyes.

"What time do you have to be up tomorrow?" I ask, leaning forward and kissing him slowly, my tongue flicking at his lips. "I'm not going to be the reason you're late for training or miss it altogether." A note of seriousness creeps into my voice.

"Champ said to be there at ten. Don't you worry about me, babe," Dirk says, running his hands down my body and resting them on my hips. "I'm going to be on time. Hell, I'm going to be early."

"Really?" I laugh. "That's not the schedule I've heard you keep."

"It hasn't been, but it will be from now on, Beth. With you in my life, I want to work harder and focus on success. I realize I've had some easy wins, but I know there's an uphill journey for me, both in the ring and with you. And I'm committed to both. I love you, Beth. It scares me how much, but I'm not running from my feelings anymore. Your love is the best prize I could ever hope to win. I love you."

My eyes fill with tears as I listen to Dirk. I cup his jaw and kiss him tenderly. "I love you, too, Dirk. And if my brother has anything to say about it, he'll have to come through me to get to you."

Dirk laughs, and it's the most perfect sound I've ever heard. "It's a deal. I'm glad I've got you in my corner. Now," he looks at me, a wicked grin on his luscious lips, "are you ready for round two?"

I push my hips against Dirk, smiling when I feel his thick cock pressing against me. "You bet I am."

EPILOGUE

"Get up here, Dirk!" Champ orders from the stage. He stands in front of the crowd, in his element with all eyes on him.

Everyone in the crowd cheers and claps as my boyfriend makes his way up to the stage.

"I wasn't sure I'd ever say this," Champ claps a hand on Dirk's back. "But you did us proud, Dirk. Congratulations on winning the fight against that lousy firefighter! I'm proud of you."

The crowd cheers again. My brother's long-standing rivalry with the captain of the fire department is well known. Though when it came out that Champ wasn't going to fight in the charity fundraiser, Doyle sent a younger guy to fight Dirk. It was a good fight, but Dirk was the winner by a mile.

Champs smiles at Dirk, who's grinning like an idiot, and slaps Dirk on the back again.

"Thanks, Champ. It means a lot to hear you say that." Dirk's voice is full of pride as he faces the crowd, but his eyes search me out. I stand a little straighter as I look at the man I love.

"And one more thing," Champ's voice booms. "Don't make me tell you to stay away from my sister again!"

Everyone laughs, and the music starts again. The Roadhouse Bar is filled with the guys from the gym and all the supporters of Champ's Gym. It's a long-running joke that he tells Dirk to stay away from me, even though we're completely committed to each other.

"Pardon me a sec, Lu," I say, wanting to congratulate Dirk again.

"No problem. Go be with your man." Luann smiles at me.

I see the longing in her eyes. I've never understood why she's still single, but she says it's part of the reason she's leaving Raytown. It never works out with the men she's dated and I know frustrates her. Raytown isn't that big and she's said it feels like she's dated all the eligible men, and some who weren't. I'm going to miss her so much when she finally leaves, but I totally understand. She deserves to find a man who makes her as happy as Dirk makes me.

I make my way through the crowd, wrapping my arms around Dirk and giving him a huge kiss.

"Get a room, you two!" Caleb yells, laughing.

I'm breathless when we stop kissing. I look into Dirk's eyes and ask, "Is Champ watching us?"

Dirk laughs, and it's the best sound in the world. "You bet your sweet curvy ass he is. He looks like his head's about to explode."

"Good." I smile. I can't help but tease my brother. He's getting used to the idea of Dirk and me together as a couple, but I know he still has doubts. But as he promised, Champ has been supportive, and I've been incredibly thankful for that.

"Save a dance for me. Okay, babe?" Dirk asks.

"Of course."

"Thanks, babe. I've gotta go talk to the boys."

I watch Dirk swagger over to Caleb and Floyd, and love fills my heart. I always wanted to believe last summer that what I shared with Dirk could be something real because it felt special. When I came back after I graduated from college, I thought it would be weird to see Dirk while I worked at the gym – and it was, but it also gave us our second chance. Now, I'm the happiest woman in the world.

"Girl, you're standing over here mooning!" Luann reaches her arm around my shoulders and hugs me.

"I can't help it," I admit, turning to face her. "There aren't words to describe this level of happiness."

"I'm so happy for you, Beth. Falling in love couldn't have happened to a better person."

"Oh, stop, Lu." I giggle, and color floods my cheeks. "It'll be you next, you know?"

"Oh, no, it won't," she responds forcefully. "I'm leaving for San Diego. I'll be a traveling nurse, and I'm going to see something of this country. I love you and everyone here in Raytown, but…"

"I understand," I tell her and give her a hug. She's told me that though she's lived in Raytown all her life, it doesn't feel quite right for her. I know she's searching for something, and I hope she finds it.

"You're not worried about Dirk?" Lu asks, pointing her chin toward Dirk and the boys as they talk and laugh.

A few of the ring girls are clustered around them, preening and trying to get their attention. Caleb puts his arms around two of the girls, clearly loving the attention and hoping to take one of them home tonight.

"No, I'm not worried," I say with one-hundred-percent certainty. "Dirk is mine. I don't have to wonder about him. He makes me feel so special and tells me he loves me every day."

"That's such a different side of Dirk. Who would've thought?"

"Yeah. I admit I had some doubts, but he shows me every day how committed he is to our relationship. He's the real deal."

"Excuse me, Luann," Dirk says, "but I need to dance with my woman."

Luann smiles and shoos us away.

Dirk leads me to the dance floor and wraps his arms around me as a slow song comes on.

"You doing alright?" I ask, smoothing his hair and planting a soft kiss on his lips.

"I'm doing all right with you in my arms." Dirk pulls me closer, and my heart overflows with love like it does every time we're together.

"That's what I like to hear."

I rest my head against his shoulder as we dance, our bodies moving perfectly. Loving Dirk is so much better than I imagined. We're a team, and nothing can divide us.

"How was work today? How was training?"

"It was cool," I say, bubbling with excitement. "They say I'm the fastest trainee for being a loan officer they've ever had. They're impressed with me."

"Of course, they're impressed with you. You're amazing, and they know it."

"Oh, stop," I joke, pretending to push him away. "You just want to get in my pants."

"I always want to get in your pants," Dirk grins and waggles his eyebrows at me, a wicked glint in his eyes. "Speaking of, when can we leave this shindig? We need to get home so I can do just that."

"Whenever you want to leave is fine with me. I'll say goodbye to Luann real quick."

"Don't take too long." Dirk's hand slides down my back to cup my ass, and my skin tickles with desire.

I pause when I see Luann talking to Caleb. From their body language, Caleb is clearly flirting with her something fierce, and Luann is lit up from within. She reaches out to touch his arm and he takes her hand and raises it to his face and slowly kisses each of her fingertips.

Good for her. Let her have some fun before she goes off on her new adventure.

I catch her eye and wink, then motion for her to call me.

By the time we make it back to my house, my skin is burning with desire for Dirk. We could barely keep our hands off each other on the drive home.

"Finally, the person I really want to celebrate with," Dirk says, his muscled arms pulling me close to his body.

"I'm incredibly proud of you, Dirk." I kiss him deeply, moaning as his hands run over my body, and he presses his thick cock against me.

We quickly make our way to my bedroom, and I almost cry at how perfect my life is. Dirk is doing well with boxing, and we're crazy happy. My brother is doing well with the gym, and I love my new job. I can't imagine a better life than the one I have now.

"I love you so much, Dirk." I open myself for the man I love, welcoming him and the pleasure only he can bring me. We're at the beginning of a lifetime together, and I look forward to every minute of it.

"I love you too, babe. I'm never letting you go."

∼

If you enjoyed this story, please rate or review on your favorite retailer, Bookbub, or Goodreads! Your feedback helps other readers find my books and lets me know which books you like best!

Prizefighter is the next book in the series! You can preorder Luann and Caleb's story at:

https://www.amazon.com/dp/B0BJ1XZWNJ

This book is part of the Heartland Heroes series. To read the full series, please visit:

https://www.amazon.com/dp/B0BFRNY6CW

Want to stay up to date on new releases, sales, and freebies! Join my newsletter!

http://eepurl.com/dh59Xr

For more Lana Love books, please visit:

https://www.amazon.com/Lana-Love/e/B078KKRB1T/

https://www.loveheartbooks.com

Printed in Great Britain
by Amazon